Instant Light

Written by Sara Maitland

Illustrations by Robert Dunn

FOREWORD

A story is often built around a kernel of truth, and the truth, if already established, lends plausibility to the fictitious. Some truths about Stockton on Tees are significant but not well known. Our ambition in the commissioning of this story is to celebrate and promote a true event; the invention of the friction match, and connect it to a current reality; the importance of festivals and events, and in particular Stockton International Riverside Festival (SIRF), to the town and the character of its inhabitants.

Maps and records from the early 19th Century suggest that a travelling circus spent the winter months on the edge of Stockton town centre, near what is now West Row. It is likely that the overwintering circus performers would have sought work in the town and become familiar figures to the town's other inhabitants. The diverse and unusual circus folk, with uncommon physical skills and artistry, may over time have become part of the culture of the area, part of its 'DNA'.

In 2012, as Stockton Council commenced work on a multi-million pound refurbishment of the town's High Street, and prepared to present the 25th SIRF, the idea emerged of a story that might form the basis of a street theatre show, and find its way into the fabric of the street. With help from New Writing North, short story writer and novelist Sara Maitland was selected and invited to produce a work which took as its starting point the invention of the friction match by John Walker in 1829.

Sara's non-realist writing is often based on old stories, myths and historic characters, and the retelling of fairy tales. Instant Light delicately weaves a story of a relationship around the world-changing but modestly exploited invention of the match, and presents us with a new tale to enjoy and retell.

It is a restless river, the Tees – it always has been. It comes dancing on the Whin Sill; hurling down the Cauldron Snout and the High Force and the Low Force; fretting away from the hills and skipping towards the sea; writhing like a serpent across the plain; and then, just when it might turn into an old and stately watercourse, it meets the tide and the new rhythms of ebb and flow, coming and going, disturb its new-found peace.

A restless river, and flowing through a restless history of Roman Legions, Viking invaders, Scottish armies, rebellious lords, dispossessed monks, hardy lead miners, iron smelters, ship builders, rope and sail and brick makers. All busy, all busy and on the move, coming up river with the tide or down river with with the spate; all a fidget of energy, of longing, of hope and restlessness.

And at the point where the down-rushing river meets the up-coming sea is a small town into which people flow like the water: sailors
and merchants and farmers and travellers.
And they mix with the folk who live
there permanently as the salt
water mixes with the
fresh. A warm yeasty
mix, restless and
changeable.

John Walker is restless too as he walks along the wide High Street in the autumn morning, with the fret coming in thick and damp and the new gas street lamps casting a sulphurous glow. He knows his neighbours think of him as a fussy little man; too nervous to be a surgeon; too prissy and private to find a wife. He knows too that they are wrong; beneath his neat coat tails and tightly curled wig he is all a fidget of energy, of ambition, of longing and restlessness. And of wasted love.

It is one or all of these which has driven him out into the night, into the fog, and now he is coming home, tired from a long walk down by the river in the dark. He is nearly 45 years old; perhaps it is too late for him, he thinks, as he passes the smart new Shambles, opened earlier in the year and it reminds him of Stephenson and the arrival of the *Locomotion* that summer. It is all new and he is old. Those are the coming men and he is the past.

Almost he fails to notice. Almost he passes by. Afterwards he does not know if it was sound or movement that caught him. But as he comes up the wide High Street something makes him glance down the dark chasm of the Ropery – the alley running westwards where the rope makers are allowed the long space they need for the un-spliced sheets that haul sails up the highest masts. For one pure and lovely moment he thinks he is seeing an angel – a winged shape dancing, whiter than the mist, flying in mid-air and his heart responds with a leaping surge of joy.

It only takes him a moment to work out what is really happening. Someone, after work the day before, had left the rope still suspended between the iron wheels (and already his mind forms a peevish tut-tut at such slovenly negligence). The damp air has shrunk the sisal and pulled the rope tight, and one of the Circus people is walking on it, or playing on it. He knows they have started to come back to town, as they come every winter, and camp out on the open ground to the west of the High Street. He has heard talk about it in his pharmacy over the last week and he is glad. Secretly he likes the Circus folk – their colourful foreign voices and raffish cheer of which he ought to disapprove, but never quite can. He loves the skill and swagger of them; the outrageous unrespectability which contrasts with his own steady demeanour. So now he clasps his hands behind his back and stands, his heels together and toes turned out as his mother taught him half a century ago and watches with deep pleasure.

The aerialist senses an audience, shifts from exercise to performance, pirouettes fast, holds an elegant arabesque perfectly still for a poised moment and then suddenly completes a running sequence of handsprings along the rope, flipping off over the iron wheel that twists the sisal into strong strands and landing on the ground not one yard away from him, hands clasped behind the back and toes turned out just like his. They both laugh. He sees it is a young woman, very dark, very slender and shockingly under-clothed. But he goes on laughing. She curtseys, sweeping low and, still moved by his angel vision, he reaches out, takes her hand and kisses it with an almost successful assumption of style. She laughs again, runs off down the High Street and disappears into the mist.

Nearly three weeks later she reappears in his shop. The young man who serves behind the counter comes back into the laboratory and says, "There is a young person outside who seems to want to see you." He says 'young person' with a sneer, and in a reflex of horror John Walker sees the young man has learned that tone from him and he is ashamed.

He does not want to leave his experiment. For some years now he has been wanting to find a way of making fire simply, quickly, on the spot – with no need to wait for sunshine and a curved glass, no need to carry a flint and tinderbox, or keep a dangerous slow fuse burning: such a simple, useful thing, but elusive, magical, mysterious. It appeals to him and he pursues it doggedly. He knows it can be done. A few years earlier a friend from his student days in York had sent him a book, translated on the wave of the Chinese fashion: *Records of the Unworldly and the Strange* by Tao Gu, written one thousand years ago. The friend knew him well, it is his sort of book and it tells him:

> An ingenious man devised the system of impregnating little sticks of pinewood with sulphur and storing them ready for use. One gets a little flame like an ear of corn. This marvellous thing was called a "light-bringing slave".

He thinks he too could be an ingenious man. So now, as in many other spare moments, he is dabbling little splinters of stick with sulphur in various compounds – with antimony and chlorate of potash and gum. These burn all right, but what is the point of a stick which burns when you touch it to a fire that is already burning – just a quick flare and a strange smell. Nothing more. Now he is laying a line of sticks out on his hearthstone, each with a chalk number corresponding to the details of the mixture neatly recorded in his notebook – the kind of fussy precision that makes people laugh at him. He does not want to see any young person, but the mirror of his sneer has shamed him and he forces a smile.

"Well, show them in," he says.

"Her" says his young man.

"Show her in."

And it is his aerialist, his dancing angel. She is smaller than he had realised, little and lithe. Pretty. Today she is wearing more clothes than that morning; in fact she is tidily though simply dressed. Her eyes slope up above her sulphur coloured cheek bones and they have smooth, flattened lids: strange and lovely to him. Perhaps like Tao Gu she is from China, but she is with the circus and all the Chinese he has ever encountered are seamen, they come on the tide, not down from the hills. His curiosity – always near the surface – bobs up with his pleasure and he smiles a welcome to her.

They cannot really speak to each other because she seems to speak no English, nor respond to his clumsy French. He tries a little Latin and catches himself wondering if Greek would be easier because it too has funny letters like Chinese, if she is Chinese.

She mimes, gesticulates, shapes a comprehensible word with her mobile fingers and suddenly he knows what she wants, what she has come for and he is very sad. "No," he says, "not me." She understands the "no" at least and the tears spring up in the corners of her sloping eyes. He cannot bear it. He reaches for a bit of paper and writes the name and address of the old woman who will, who does, who says "yes."

For one moment she lowers her head and looks so terribly sad that he wants to explain to her that for him it is not a moral issue, he just cannot bear to be so close to injured bodies, to cut into them, to touch so intimately and to hurt;

that is why he gave up his training as a surgeon and became a more humble pharmacist instead. But then her mood changes like the moment she changed from poised stillness to the glorious springing head-over-heels of that morning in the Ropery – and she picks up three little mortars from his table and starts to juggle with them, so clearly displaying and performing her gratitude that no words are needed. The rounded mortars skip and fly through the air like she had done; she reaches out for another and turning round he opens the cupboard so that she can see a full row of the pots. She circles the table without missing a beat and starts adding to her act: five, six, eight little clay bowls whizzing around his usually sober laboratory, catching the light, a water fall, a rising tide of movement and joy. When she reaches out for yet another it becomes harder; he feels her tense a little, step backwards, watching not her own hands but the very highest point of her cascade.

As she settles the new flow of them she steps backwards and her heel catches one of his tipped shards of pine wood, grinding it against the rough hearth-stone and it sparks into life. She is startled, but unfazed . . . she glances down swiftly then holds out her skirt and the pots fall into her lap. But he is not watching this; he is on his knees, his wig askew, looking at the bright little flame like an ear of corn.

Punctiliously he notes the chalk number then picks up the stick next to the flaming one and pulls it across the stone – and it too sparks, shimmers into unexpected light. Instant fire. He tries some more – some of them do not burn and with one there is a tiny explosion and the burning head darts across the room and lands smouldering on the rug; but with the pots still in her skirts and a transfixed look on her face she stamps it out, while he notes that number too. At least half the little sticks give birth to fire, fire from friction.

Very solemnly he stands up, bows to her as she had curtsied to him before and says, "We have invented the friction match; we have brought instant light and fire to humanity."

Her laughter and delight peel around the room. She unloads the pots onto the floor, returns his obeisance with a deep sweep and claps her hands in applause. He gives her a little stick and in her turn she strikes it against the stone and laughs again as the flame spurts out.

17

He goes to the table, picks up a quill and writes the date and the chalk number in his notebook. Then he writes *vici* – "I conquered" and signs it, "John Walker." He smiles. After a moment he crosses out *vici* and writes *vicimus* instead – "we conquered." He offers her the quill and points to the space below his name. She hesitates and then scrawls an X.

"John Walker," he says and points at himself. Then he points at her and she smiles shyly and says, "Vesta."

It is only as he writes it down beside her X that he remembers that Vesta is the goddess of fire in the hearth, the domestic flame. Slowly he goes to the cupboard again and takes out his cash box and opens it. He reaches careful fingers into the pocket of her skirt and takes out the little scrap of paper he had given her earlier, offering her the open box and an interrogative expression. She smiles a deep solemn smile, quite different from the merry smiles of before; she takes the paper back from him, picks up one more little stick from the hearth, strikes it and sets fire to the scrap, letting the ashes fall slowly to the ground. Then she goes to the box and takes a couple of coins, leaving the rest undisturbed.

A few days later she comes into the chemist's shop again. She gives him a tiny packet and watches as he unwraps it. It is a small piece of card folded in half and when he opens it he can see that it is sandpaper. He looks at it, baffled; she laughs again, goes through into the laboratory, picks up a new fire-stick, slips it between the fold of the card and pulls sharply: the tip of the stick ignites with a little hiss and burns steadily. She takes another stick and the little striking paper and tucks it into his breast pocket. It is his turn to laugh.

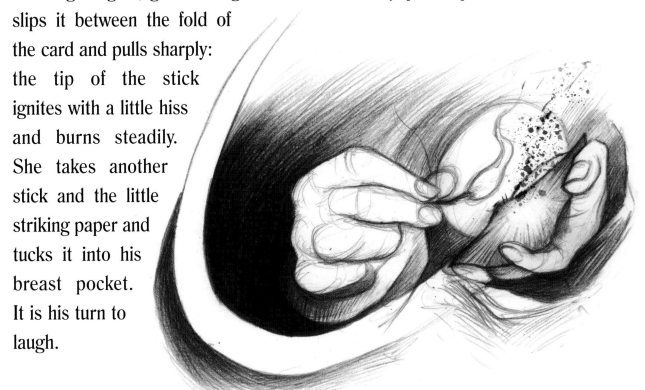

Now whenever she visits he leaves the cash box open on the table and she takes what she needs, never very much and he never counts. Sometimes she juggles for him. Always they smile, often they laugh and all winter he is happy.

Just as the catkins are swelling on the hazel bushes, a tall man knocks on his front door in the earliest grey hour of a morning. He goes down in his nightcap and the man says, "She says to ask you to come."

He gets dressed, pulls his wig on, washes his hands and goes out, along the Ropery – stepping carefully over the piles of sisal and coils – to the shanty village on the west side of the town. There, overcoming his aversion to bodily procedures, and striking light from the small sticks he always carries in his pocket, to the stunned amazement of the women who are gathered with her, he helps her deliver her baby son.

The child spends its first days in the laboratory, as she pops in and out from her rehearsals.

"Is that child yours?" asks his sister sternly.

"No," he says indignantly, but afterwards he wishes he had been bold enough to say, "Yes. Sort of."

Three weeks later she comes to say goodbye, standing up on tip-toe to kiss his cheek. She laughs and he cries a little.

"Will you come back?"

She nods, takes the child and is gone.

It is a good summer. The fire-sticks catch on – he sells them in boxes of 50 and each box comes with a little folded piece of sandpaper, so they can be lit even in the rain. His neighbours are impressed and no longer think of him as a fussy little man, but as a scientist and inventor. The great Michael Faraday comes all the way from London to discuss experimental chemistry and advise him, most sincerely, to patent his invention. He cannot do that of course, because it is not just his, but he does not explain this. He just nods and shrugs. Even his sister is civil after that visit.

When the autumn mists return and the fret rolls in from the sea again, he makes his preparations. He decides to enlist poor boys from the town to help him soak long strands of thin rope in pitch and carefully mixed chemicals and then drape them from the roof tops, over the Shambles and the Town Hall, high above the market and the broad roadway – a complex spider's web of fine cords. He keeps an ear to the ground and hears when the Circus folk are approaching. So when she comes dancing down the Ropery with the child in her arms, he blows sharply on a whistle and each lad runs to his place and lights his rope with a fire-stick. Suddenly all the High Street is a sparkling, exploding, dancing fire show of noise and light, and flames and sparks – red, orange, yellow, green, blue, purple, gold and silver.

And she lifts the baby high to see the show and she laughs and laughs and laughs.

Every year when the Circus folk come down the valley, along the restless river, he makes a new show to welcome them. And when the lad gets big enough, he and his friends reciprocate; they explode out of the Ropery, tumbling, juggling, stilt walking, clowning, drumming, singing, performing.

Each year more people come to enjoy it. The show grows and flourishes until the citizens of the small town where the down-rushing river meets the up-coming tide forget why they are lighting fireworks and putting on shows and welcoming strangers. They just do it and enjoy it. They barely notice the old man in an old fashioned wig and the middle aged woman with the strangely sloping eyes who stand outside the chemist's shop on the High Street, watching the show, holding hands and laughing.

JOHN WALKER 1781-1859

John Walker was born on 29 May 1781
at 104 High Street, Stockton.

At about the age of fifteen John Walker was apprenticed to Mr. Watson Alcock, a surgeon who was physician to the Marquis of Londonderry. However he did not remain in this profession for long and it has been suggested that he could not stand the sight of blood!

In 1819 John opened a shop as a "chymist and druggist" at 59 High Street, which had a workshop to the rear of the shop where he carried out his experiments. A lot of his experimental work was with light-producing agents, including phosphorus. His breakthrough came in 1826-27 whilst he was working at home with a combustible paste - he knew the mixture would flare-up but was not explosive. The eureka moment came when he scraped the mixing stick on the hearth at his home and it "spluttered and caught fire".

By 1827 John Walker was selling these "friction lights", or matches, to the public at 1s 2d (6 new pence) per 100, in a tin case with piece of sandpaper to ignite them. These matches were very popular in the town, with one early customer being the Stockton to Darlington Railway, but their fame soon spread. John did not patent his invention as he was keen it should benefit mankind, other inventors were not so benevolent. Thus with other brands, especially "Lucifers", rapidly gaining a well established market, John ceased production in the early 1830s. John Walker continued to trade as a chemist until he retired and sold the business in 1858, but unfortunately died the following year.